DAIRY TRIALS

Complete Dark Hucow BDSM Series

Leandra Camilli

ISBN: 9798370537486
Imprint: Independently published

1st edition

CONTENTS

HUCOW FLAVOR

CHAPTER 1

It was a failure. I was a failure. No matter how much I tried to say otherwise, I was that and couldn't do anything about it. Every time I thought about changing myself, I always came to the same conclusion.

Going to college had been a mistake. I would never do it again, I promised myself.

I was in my shitty apartment, looking at myself in the mirror. If there was at least something about me that still was a reason to feel proud of myself, it was my looks. People always complimented me about them, and it would never be different.

Not to mention that I was only 22 and fresh out of college. People often went to college to get amazing and well-paying jobs, but it wasn't the case for me.

It wasn't the case for me because I took and finished a major in writing, and even though I learned a lot, I couldn't make much money from my books. They were all short stories because I was afraid of writing longer books.

Nothing I could do about that.

Turning around, I found myself in the living room. At least here in my apartment, I had privacy. I had the privacy to do what I wanted to do, and it was like a drug to me.

Finding my dildo, I held it in my hand. It was painted to resemble skin, was veiny, and even had a function to make it vibrate. In other words, it was a vibrator.

Even though I had already used it several times, I felt ashamed of it because I was still a virgin. Not much I could do about that other than to lament, I thought, putting the vibrator on the floor and lowering myself on it.

Another good thing about living by myself was that I could walk around in my apartment naked. I didn't even have to worry about the neighbors spying on me. Most men around here didn't think I was hot, after all.

Imagine that.

I didn't know what it was with the men around here, but they never looked twice at me.

They were all looking for more experienced, older women and I didn't fit in that category.

Not only was I 22, but I also looked younger than my age, and people always said that about me. There was also something about me that they always mentioned, and it was my small boobs.

Anyway, I shouldn't be thinking about those things. I should be focusing on easing the dildo into my pussy. I swear, every time this happened, there was something different about it. It always made me feel something different, and this time it was going to be just like that.

I could already feel it. I could feel it going inside of me, and I was already feeling breathless.

"Oh God," I murmured, wishing that the vibrator was actually a cock and a man was doing this to me. It was a pity that it would never happen. Nothing about that I could do, I thought before bobbing on the vibrator, feeling it stretching my walls.

It was like the first time I was doing this, even though it wasn't.

A few minutes later, I came, my juice coming out while my nipples went stiff. I began to play with them, twirling and tugging them.

After a while, I came one more time, my body shaking with pleasure. I had never felt so much pleasure as I was feeling now, or maybe I had already felt something similar and just couldn't remember it right now. Considering the hit of dopamine in my mind, that wasn't an impossibility.

By the time it was all over, I couldn't even remember where I was anymore. I pushed myself up and left the vibrator on the floor, glancing at the puddle that I left. I would clean it later.

After that, I clambered onto the couch, sitting on it. My eyes noticed a newspaper on a small table, and I picked it up. Holding it in my hands, I flipped the pages until I found what I was looking for, which was actually anything that could entertain me for a little while.

An ad on the page caught my attention and I began to read what it said.

If you're looking for the biggest opportunity of your life, you might have just found it. We are from the Dairy Club and we are looking to invite someone special to join it, and all you would have to do is to give up your body for us.

We would be able to do whatever we want.

The words piqued my interest. I only had to offer up my body? I asked myself, checking the ad a little more carefully this time.

What I read was true. The ad mentioned the part about giving up my body for the members of the Dairy Club, and I couldn't help but think it just might be the opportunity I was looking for.

Especially because of this one part in the ad that resonated with me.

You will be paid handsomely, though we do think that when you come here, you will find out that you don't want to leave this place at all.

Whoever they were, they were pretty assured of themselves, and I found myself so interested in the ad that I just wanted to log into their website and sign up.

After reading the last part of the ad, though, I soon found out that it said that I needed to send a letter.

Send a letter? I asked myself, finding that a little unusual, but still deciding to take the plunge.

I mean, what else was I going to do? My life was shit and I didn't have any other possible opportunities for my future, so I might as well just sign up for the Dairy Club.

Still, I didn't think that I was going to become a full-fledged member or anything of the sort. If anything, they were only going to do what they mentioned in the ad.

The part about using my body however they wanted…

CHAPTER 2

After I signed up and sent the letter, I received the confirmation in another letter, and it was fancy and there was a nice smell coming from it.

That was unusual.

But I didn't think much of it. At the time, my heart was beating like a jackhammer, and I was shocked more than anything that I was accepted into the Dairy Club.

They were going to turn me into a hucow. That was also another thing mentioned in the ad.

My heart was already speeding up just thinking about it.

A few hours after I received the confirmation letter, someone in a limousine picked me up in front of my dingy apartment block.

All my neighbors and the people that I despised the most watched me climb into the limousine, most of them foaming at the mouth.

They thought that I had turned things around in my life and that I had a lot more money than they had. Even though it was the wrong assumption about where my life was heading, I still enjoyed it a lot more than I should have.

It was a few minutes after that, and now I found myself in front of the huge house that was more like a mansion. A sprawling, imposing mansion that made me feel small, which was a first.

I was lost here, though.

I thought that someone was going to greet me at the front

door, but so far, no one appeared. But I did hear some sound coming from the other side of the mansion, and my interest couldn't help but be piqued.

Was someone swimming? I asked myself, deciding to go there right away. I had to. There was no other way. If someone was swimming, I couldn't help but find out who he was, and how hot he was, too. Could be a woman, too, but my gut said that it was a man.

My pussy was begging for me to do that, and that was putting it mildly.

I certainly wasn't exaggerating.

A few moments later, I found myself on the other side of the house, seeing the man swimming. Woah. Even from afar, there was no denying that he was hot. *Mouthwateringly so.* His muscles seemed to dance under the sunlight, which shone brightly on the skin.

If before my pussy was begging for me to be here, now it was pleading for me to go closer. But how could I go closer, considering that I didn't want his attention on me and him finding out that I was here and didn't follow the 'protocol'? I asked myself.

There was no turning back anymore, so I decided to take a few steps toward him. His arms were still creating waves in the water and splashing it, and he was going from one side of the swimming pool to the other.

I didn't know much about swimming, but it appeared that he was a professional.

If not that, then he should certainly consider himself a professional swimmer, I thought.

The moment I took another step toward him, he turned in the water, his eyes quickly finding me. I knew it was going to happen, but I was still taken aback by it, and for a moment, I didn't know what to say or what to do.

I just kept on wringing my hands, wondering what he was going to say.

Even from afar, it was obvious that he was a significant number of years older than me, and I wasn't exaggerating.

After all, the wrinkles and the white in his hair showed me as much.

And that meant he was even more of a turn-on for me, so much so that my body grew hotter just thinking about what we could do.

What we could do? I asked myself, realizing how ridiculous that was. Chances were that nothing was going to happen between us, not to mention that, if he was a member of the Dairy Club, then he didn't want me snooping around.

He was going to punish me, wasn't he? I thought the moment he waved his hand above the water. He was so far from me that he would have to shout so that I could hear him, and I assumed that he wasn't someone to do that.

I took a deep breath the moment he pulled himself out of the water, the water flowing down on it, the muscles shining under the sunlight.

And now that he was out of the water, his body looked even hotter, and I wasn't exaggerating. I found myself wishing to be with my hands sliding over every line and every curve of his. Just looking at him was enough to make me shudder with delight.

"I didn't think you were going to come so soon. One of the guys must have approved your delivery here before I could even check the documents," he said and his voice was even sexier than the man himself. It melted my body.

For a moment, I didn't even know what to say. What was I supposed to say, anyway? I asked myself, him closer to me now. The fact he was so close to me meant I could smell his scent, and it destroyed me internally, even more so than I already was.

It was ridiculous. I didn't even know what to do and how to proceed, and I only knew that I wanted to feel his muscles with my hands and worship him.

Without even signing any document, I was already submitting myself to his whims and pleasures. The man knew that just from looking at me, too.

I didn't need to glance down to know that he was sporting a huge boner in his speedo. Gosh, the size of that bulge was too much for me to handle, and in a moment, I… passed out.

I didn't even know how it happened. One moment I was with him by the swimming pool, and the next I was on the tiles, my body splayed on it.

CHAPTER 3

My eyes fluttering open, I found myself where I imagined I was going to be. I was in a study room, lying on a comfortable and old-school couch. Looking at the ceiling, I could see the fan spinning. It was doing so slowly and even though it looked old, it wasn't creaking or making any other noises.

"Here. This is going to make you feel better," the voice from the same man from before said and upon turning my eyes to the right, I found a glass of whiskey in front of me.

Flicking my eyes up, I found him, and he was wearing nothing more than what he was wearing before. He only had his blue speedo on, standing no more than a couple of inches from me.

The study room where we were was quiet, so much so that I could even hear his breathing. It was unsettling, but at the same time, incredibly alluring to what was going to happen.

I couldn't just look at the whiskey without doing something with it, so I chugged it down, feeling the alcohol warming me up.

I felt better but was still shocked by the development of these events.

"Thanks. I needed it," I admitted, not knowing what to do. His body was just so perfect, almost like he was a god himself. Especially now that he turned his back to me so that he picked up something from a small table, I noticed that even more strongly than before.

My body was like a furnace, the temperature increasing evermore.

Turning back around, I noticed he was showing me a couple of documents.

"I thought that we were going to start this by properly introducing ourselves, but after talking with the guys, I think that we can already skip the best part," he said, his eyes studying me carefully. I felt that he was freezing me up just with his stare, and I truly couldn't do anything out of fear. "These documents will seal your life for the Dairy Club. After signing under the fine print, you will be ours forever."

I couldn't help but gulp, wondering what was going to happen now. If I signed where he wanted me to sign, what would happen then? Would I be able to say no if I didn't want what would happen?

The moment I was going to open my mouth to ask him about that, he responded, "these documents are important, but in case you ever change your mind, you can always do so. I assure you that it will never happen, though."

I didn't have enough time to read the entire set of documents, even though part of me nagged me about doing that. I just took the document from his hand, signed where I needed to sign with his pen, and then delivered them back to him.

After that, I took a deep breath in.

What was going to happen now? I asked myself, my body trembling with fear and excitement. Whatever had to happen from this moment onward, it was going to be filled with milking sessions, and he and his friends would even fuck me.

Finally, I felt appreciated. That was the word I was looking for, and it fitted this moment to perfection.

Checking my signature one last time, he put the documents back down on the small table, leering at me.

"It's perfect," he said, puzzling me.

"What do you mean by 'it's perfect?'" I asked, wondering if he was going to be truthful about the answer.

"We can already start everything, and I'm going to be the one to fuck you first," he promised, not doing anything after that. He was looking for consent, and I could only nod after putting the empty glass on the small table by my side.

Time to enter my submissive state of mind.

"Yes, Master. Do whatever you want to do to me." And after saying that, I took a deep breath in. There was even something even more important that needed to be said, too. "I'm a virgin. I think that's something you should know about me."

"You are a virgin?" He asked, smirking. "For some reason, I already knew that. You didn't even need to say anything about it. It was written on your face."

I didn't know what he meant by it being written on my face, but my mind was obsessing over all the possible outcomes of my decision.

He was a member of the Dairy Club and all the members in it had equal shares of my body, and yet, he was going to be the one to fuck me first. I couldn't stop obsessing over that.

It wasn't even that. It was something else.

He also had a whiskey glass he was holding in his hand, but he put it back down on a small table the moment he noticed the direction this was taking. There was still some whiskey in it.

Now that both of his hands were free, he offered me his right hand, saying, "stand up with me. I want to dance with you."

Dance with me? I asked myself, my body feeling tingles of pleasure. It felt that because the way he was holding my hand now, after I took his, was sending all the right signals in me, and I wasn't exaggerating.

He hadn't even started the right tunes for this moment.

When he also noticed the quietness in the study room, he went to the radio on a small table and pressed the play button. Coming over to me, he took both of my hands, and we started to move following the rhythm of the tunes.

They were slow, and for the time being, he wasn't even saying anything. Not yet, anyway.

I just remembered that he hadn't told me his name yet. When was he going to do that?

CHAPTER 4

As if he could read my mind, he said, "I know your name is Stacy. It's a pretty name. I'm Jeremy."

Jeremy. I was going to keep his name in mind, I thought and for the next two minutes, we just continued to dance following the rhythm of the tunes. They remained unchanged. Slow and comforting.

It was as though Jeremy decided to play this music to ease me into this moment and remove my nervousness.

If that was the case, it was working. A few moments after we started to dance to the music, my heart stopped racing.

When the music ended, he said, "you dance well, but that's not why you came here. You came here to be my pretty little plaything, and that's exactly what you are going to become." Giving it a moment of silence, he added, "it isn't going to happen here, though. I have a better place."

A sex dungeon.

I didn't even have to ask him if that was what it was. He turned with me and we made our way to the basement, in a moment finding ourselves in a dark room with candelabra on the walls. The candle lights flickering in the darkness, I couldn't help but feel shivers running down my spine.

This was the darkest sex dungeon I had seen in my life, and I wasn't exaggerating.

It was also littered with all kinds of toys. I was going to be more than his plaything. He was going to torment me through wave after wave of pleasure.

My whole body grew hotter just thinking about it.

Jeremy put his hand on my left shoulder, guiding me to the other side of the dungeon. There was a button on the wall and he pressed it. After that, a portion of the wall slid to the side, revealing a small and metallic chamber. It was big enough to fit a full person in it.

"Step inside. This chamber is what will transform you," Jeremy announced, making me stay right where I was. If the chamber was what was going to transform me into a hucow, how was it going to work?

The moment I was going to turn my head and open my mouth to ask him about that, he replied, "and don't worry about it. The transformation will be seamless."

I didn't know about that, but my eyes were still set on something else.

Before I could step into the chamber, he applied pressure on my shoulder with his fingers, making me stop.

"Before you do that, though, take off your clothes. You have to be naked in there."

For a moment, I didn't know if I was going to proceed or not, but then I made up my mind and began to undress.

One piece after the other, I shed off my clothes, finding myself naked in front of Jeremy. I couldn't look over my shoulder, but I was still pretty certain that he was eyeing me from top to bottom. His eyes were scrutinizing every part of me.

I even felt as if it was something physical.

Nudging me slightly, I stepped into the chamber, and after turning around, he pressed the same button to close the door. It was filled with some kind of gas that knocked me out in an instant, and surprisingly, some supports prevented me from falling down to the floor.

Moments later, I reopened my eyes and still found myself inside the chamber, but this time, my body was different. It was much bigger and more curvaceous, and I immediately felt some slight pain coming from my boobs. They were already producing milk, and I knew that my master was already thinking about milking me.

He was probably even going to do so with his mouth instead of the milking machine. I'd seen it when I stepped into his sex dungeon.

In the meantime, I also couldn't help but wonder when the rest of the members of the Dairy Club would come here.

He pressed the same button and the door in front of me opened. Stepping outside, I realized that my body was so much bigger that it also weighed a lot more. Walking had become more difficult; I wasn't going to deny it.

No wonder why he demanded that I undress, I thought.

Fearing I was going to fall down to the floor, he held me with his strong hands, still leering at me.

"My goodness. When my buddies and I thought about starting this club, I didn't think that our first subject was going to be a beauty like you. There are so many things I want to do to you."

I didn't even know what to say, just that I was surprised that he was complimenting me so much from the start. I wanted to look at myself in a mirror, and it was a pity that there were no mirrors nearby.

For a moment, I thought that he was going to kiss me, but he was only scrutinizing every part of me with his hungry eyes. Just like in the study room, the sex dungeon was silent, and I could hear his breathing, and also mine.

One thing I was beginning to notice about my body, now that I was a hucow, was that thanks to its bigger size, it took a lot more from me than usual to move it. I was beginning to suspect I was going to have to start to eat a lot more starting from now.

"I'm not going to kiss you now, darling," he murmured, his hands going around me and cupping my ass cheeks.

I knew he was going to do that, but it still sent ripples of pleasure through my body, and I melted. All the strength in my legs faded away, and I soon found myself exactly where he wanted me to be.

On my knees and with his big, veiny dick standing proudly in front of me. While I was in the chamber, he must have taken off his speedo, which was good news and a pity at the same time.

I had actually been hoping to see him doing that.

CHAPTER 5

It was as though Jeremy could read my mind. I was in a completely submissive position, so much so that I didn't say anything when he clamped a collar around my neck and locked my wrists with a pair of handcuffs.

Now, I was bound and he felt more comfortable doing anything he wanted to me, more so than ever before.

He proceeded to the other side of the sex dungeon, picking up something. It was metallic and small. I didn't need to think about it too hard to know what it was. It was a butt plug.

Wait, he wasn't only going to take the virginity of my pussy, but also of my asshole? My body was already shuddering thinking about that. I was thinking about him filling all of my holes, stretching me to my absolute limits.

"Bend down and accept this," he ordered and I had no choice but to obey, splaying the upper portion of my body on the cold floor made of stones, waiting for him to squeeze the butt plug into my ass.

He walked until he stood behind me, proceeding to stick the butt plug inside. Feeling it coming inside, I couldn't help but grimace and shut my eyes until they were like slits, pain flaring up in me. I never thought it was possible to feel so much pain.

"Ahhh, and there's also something interesting about this butt plug that I'm sure you're going to love to know," he announced before producing a small remote. There were only a few buttons on it, and he pressed one of them. The moment he did that, a jolt of electricity shot through me, making my body shake and tremble.

And even though it was alarming as much as it was shocking, it rewarded me with a lot more pleasure than I thought possible, my body sweating. I was huffing, too.

Not much I could do about that.

"Holy shit. I almost passed out again," I confessed, which would have been a disappointment to me. I didn't want to pass out and miss the most important part of this.

"There are so many things we are going to do to you after this introduction," Jeremy promised, and I couldn't help but feel fear and excitement at the same time.

The butt plug was inside of my ass, and I just wanted it there for all of eternity, even though I knew it was an impossibility. Eventually, it would have to be plucked out of me, and after that, he would take my virginity.

I would feel so complete when that happened.

Taking a deep breath, I was readying myself to suck his mesmerizing, hallucinating dick when he threw me to the side, turning me around. He mounted me and bent down, his lips seeking one thing – or rather, two of them. My boobs.

They were already aching with the milk stored in them, and some of it was even leaking. I couldn't do anything about that. I felt it was a pity to see the drops coming out. They deserved to be stored in the proper place, either to be sold or in his stomach. I was sure that Jeremy was already thirsty for it, after all.

Flicking his eyes up, he said, "you have no idea how much I've been waiting for this."

After saying that, he latched his lips around my right nipple, and he started to apply pressure and suck it. The milk stored in my right boob began to come out, and a wave of relief washed over me.

It was too much. So much so that I closed my eyes and started to rub my clit, wishing to bring myself to my climax.

I could feel it coming. I even began to grind my body against his as I followed his pace, and I thought it was going to happen. After all, my body was growing hot and it was becoming increasingly more difficult to breathe.

In the midst of all that, Jeremy was still milking and sucking me. I almost thought that he could never empty me.

But just when I thought my orgasm was going to wash over me, he grabbed my hand, stopping my masturbation. Opening my eyes, I had to ask him what he thought he was doing.

Then, Jeremy responded, "what? You thought it was going to be so easy?" He sniffled me slowly and sensually, the light coming from the candelabra shifting over his muscles. "Not a chance. If anything, the next time you try something like that, I will put a cage on you. I already have full control over your body, and from this moment onward, you can only do everything and anything I want. This is certainly not an equal relationship, my dear."

I gulped. I already knew that, but it was still different, hearing it from him.

Anyway, my mind wasn't even focused on that. Rather, it was focused on his next goal, which was my other nipple. He gave it a glance before latching his lips around it, and then the sucking started, and it went on for like an eternity.

The fact he was mounted on me made me feel small, more so than usual.

Trembling, I thought that I was going to come without masturbating myself, but then Jeremy pulled his head back. It caused a plop that echoed in the darkness of his sex dungeon.

Locking my eyes with his, I opened my mouth, but then he clamped his hand on it, stopping me.

"I don't want you to say anything. In fact, I think that now I'm going to take all of your virginities, and you will thank me for it."

I smiled.

There was no promise better than that one, and it already excited me beyond my limits.

CHAPTER 6

And he did. He showed me he was going to do that. With his cock in his hand, he knew what to do. He took a step forward and allowed me to latch my lips around the gland. I was losing the virginity of my mouth, and I felt a surge of pleasure coursing through my entire body, thinking about that.

But it wasn't the only thing I was thinking about. In fact, I was thinking about something else. I was obsessing over how good his gland felt between my lips, and it was just that. Just the gland and nothing else. I was swirling and moving my tongue around it, savoring the taste of his pre-cum. It was delicious.

I began to bob up and down, getting greedier and putting more inches into my mouth. I was getting bold, too, and I even started to fondle his balls, enjoying every second. His balls were heavy and laden with his sperm, and I could only wonder for how long he would be shooting out his load inside of me. It just couldn't go anywhere.

I was getting so greedy that I thought that the status quo wasn't going to change and he was only going to come into my mouth, but he then pushed me away from him with his hand on my forehead.

I couldn't help but look up, wondering what was going on in his mind. I thought that he wanted me to make him come into my mouth.

"I know that it hasn't been long yet, but I have something else I want to do. I think that you are ready for it," he explained before going behind me and plucking the butt plug out.

I knew he was going to do that, but I still felt like I was missing a limb. It was a feeling that would only be sated when he penetrated me with his shaft, and I was already waiting for him to do that.

"Nobody in the Dairy Club will be happy when they find out about this, but fuck it. I don't care about what they think. I'm going to come inside of you and knock you up. That's what you want too, right?"

I nodded once and frantically. What else was I supposed to do? The thought of him coming inside of me and knocking me up sent shivers of pleasure through my body.

But the fact that he plucked out the butt plug meant he planned on doing something else, which was to take the virginity of my asshole.

And I was already waiting for that. Jeremy then mounted me from behind, sliding his prick in there. He was so wet and slick from the blowjob he didn't even need to use lube for this. His manhood slotted inside with no difficulty.

And it stretched my walls down there in ways I never thought possible, and I could only clench my jaw and grit my teeth.

Never before had I felt so much pleasure and was so horny. I thought I was going to explode.

"Oh God, oh God," I could only mutter over and over, not knowing if and when I was going to come, only that it was going to happen.

"Fuck, you are so tight," he murmured behind me, rolling his hips a moment later. As he did that, his balls slapped against my butt, the noises echoing in the sex dungeon.

Just outside, I heard car doors closing, and I couldn't help but wonder who was coming.

Either way, it wasn't at the forefront of my thoughts, so I didn't care about it much.

My mind was focused on the way that his balls were slapping against me and if he'd lied about knocking me up. He could unload his sperm inside my rectum, and it would be rewarding, but it would not be the same thing as him knocking me up.

Most of all, I just wanted his heir.

Thinking about that, I couldn't stop it when it finally happened. It broke through every barrier I had set up for it, and it made my body shake and thrash about with raw lust, my climax finally erupting.

When the time was over, I was breathless and I could barely keep myself awake. I thought I was going to pass out thanks to the overwhelming sensations that our sex brought to us.

Jeremy pulled out of me with a pop, his dick glistening. It shone under the light from the candelabra. He moved around me and positioned himself in front of me.

The first thought that crossed my mind was that he wanted me to give him another blowjob, but the way that he pushed me down until I was lying on my back showed me otherwise.

He mounted me and pried open my pussy with his fingers, not doing anything for the next few seconds.

"This is going to be our dirty little secret and, outside of this club, you can't tell anyone about it, not that I think you will ever leave the estate," he demanded and I could only nod. Whatever he wanted me to do, I was going to do it.

Then, he slotted his prick inside my pussy, popping my hymen. Rolling his hips again, he pounded me against the floor, drawing this out for as long as he could.

I closed my eyes and began to moo. Not moan or groan. I mooed, my nails running on his back and I threw my legs around him. I was doing everything in my power to keep him locked tight to me, and it was working.

By the time it was all over, he unloaded his milk inside of me, and I could feel it filling me with it. It was all so great that we came together, and this was an experience that I would never forget.

"Jesus, this was better than I thought," he admitted before jamming his prick inside of me one last time to make sure that not a single drop was going to be wasted, and none was.

Then, he gave my forehead a peck and pulled out.

Panting, I passed out. I had no idea what was going to happen later, but I would certainly meet the other members of the club. They had to be already waiting for me.

EPILOGUE

When I came back to my senses, I wasn't in the sex dungeon anymore, but rather in the living room. It was spacious and welcoming, and I could see myself spending hours here without getting bored.

I could see that happening often here, especially now that I lived in this estate. I couldn't imagine myself going anywhere, to be honest.

I was lying on the couch, and I sat up on it when I realized that there was no one around. Not even the butlers and other employees.

My head was a little heavy, though. Upon turning my eyes left and right, trying to find out what happened since I passed out, I began to hear some people whispering not too far away, and I couldn't help but wonder who they were.

Whoever they were, they were coming this way, though. After all, I could hear their footsteps approaching where I was.

I straightened up my spine. One of the reasons why I did that was that I was naked. So, if they weren't members of the Dairy Club, they would cause a scene here, freaking out after seeing me, and I wanted to avoid that.

I just loved the quietness that was settled in the living room.

"There she is. As you can see, she's already a hucow," Jeremy explained, pointing his index finger at me. He was with some other guys, and I noticed that they were very similar to him, and another thing was that they didn't look surprised after seeing me.

I thought that my being naked was going to freak them out.

Lifting my hand, I said, "hi. I'm Stacy and I'm so happy to see you. You are members of the Dairy Club too, right?"

They all nodded. There were three of them, Jeremy included.

Glancing down, I couldn't help but notice the boners in their pants. No reason to think they weren't members of the Dairy Club. In fact, I was beginning to think that they came here for only one purpose, which was to fuck me.

My mouth was already salivating just thinking about that.

"And you're telling me that she is only 22?" One of the members of the club asked, making me wonder who he was.

I supposed that was something I would find out soon.

HOLLYWOOD
HUCOW SHARED

CHAPTER 1

I could see them following me from a distance. They thought they were hidden by the darkness that encroached on us, but they were mistaken. I could see them in the reflections on the puddles, too.

They were leering at me, thinking that I would never confront them about this. But they were so mistaken about it.

I was going to do that and a lot more starting tonight.

But maybe it wasn't going to happen now. Maybe I was going to wait until it was the right moment to strike.

After all, tonight I decided to come with something I had in my purse. I had been trained to use it, so unless they planned on doing something about that beforehand, it wasn't going to work.

Taking a deep breath, I headed down the stairs to the part under the buildings. In no moment at all, I found myself in the parking lot. It being underground meant all the noise about to be generated here was going to be contained, and I would rather have things that way.

I just didn't want to risk anything was what I was saying.

Turning around, I found the first guy entering the parking lot after me, and there was no denying he'd already been suspecting that I was going to lead them down here.

They had all always thought that I was going to find out about what they were doing.

I shouted, "whatever you think you are doing, I'm going to call the police. I already have everything ready."

And after warning them with that, I took my phone out of my purse and held it in front of me, my fingers trembling.

I couldn't deny that this was instilling fear in me, more so than I thought it was going to.

The other men showed up, also leering as much as the first guy. They thought they were sexy, didn't they? I asked without externalizing that. Doing so wouldn't help me no matter how much I tried to.

"We don't care about the police," the first man said and I couldn't help but wonder if his voice wasn't one that I'd already heard before. Maybe in a TV show or something like that. Whatever the case, it wasn't going to change my mind about what I was doing, especially considering that there was no turning back anymore.

After I showed them that I was aware they were following me, now it was time to finish this before it was too late.

"You should. I'm going to destroy your life with them. You know that tailing people is wrong, right?"

He chuckled. I imagined he was going to do that, and I wasn't surprised by it.

"Neither of us thinks that something like that can happen. No matter how you try to frame it, it's not going to work and it won't scare us," the first guy said.

Him being the only one talking right now made me feel that he was the leader of the group. Three men. It would be difficult for me to fight against them, but they couldn't scare me.

Dialing 911, I put my phone on my ear the moment the guy in the middle said again, "you should hang up now before it's too late. We know someone pretty important to you, and we want to talk about a proposition he made to us."

Someone important to me? I couldn't help but wonder who that person was, and maybe now was the right moment to ask about that and dig up a little bit more about what was happening here.

"Who are you talking about?" I asked, hoping for a brief answer, but none came.

Not yet, anyway.

"Your husband," he replied a couple of seconds after that. "John."

"John? What does he have to do with this?"

I didn't like that. The direction this was taking was creating fear in me, and I didn't know what to do with it.

"He lost in a bet and thinks that you are the only one that can save him."

"He thinks that I'm the only one that can save him?" I asked, finding that unbelievable. Without a shred of doubt, this had to mean that these guys were only playing with me, right? It couldn't be anything else.

"He lost in a game big time and you have to do something about that, and we think you should offer us something, the only thing that you have and what you've been thinking about for so long."

Huh? I needed to focus on something else right now. I couldn't do this out of order.

"Before we even continue to talk about this, I want to know your names."

I wanted to know where this was going, especially if I was to give him something that only I could offer up.

"I'm Jeremy, and these are Robert and Edward. We are sorry that this is happening this way, but I thought that we should be upfront about it."

"About what?" I probed. I took that they already knew my name. I don't have to tell them what it was.

"About you joining the Dairy Club," he explained without showing any emotion on his face, which only made this feel creepier than it already was. I even felt shivers running down my spine, something that didn't happen often. I prided myself in being braver than most people.

"Joining the Dairy Club?" I asked, not even understanding why there was this instant connection between those two words. There was something about them I couldn't quite describe and I wanted to know more about them. "What's that?"

"It's a club where we perform some explorations and studies on women like you, and we think that you would be a great addition to the herd."

"Herd?" I let out, not even knowing what to think about that.

So, he thought that I was like a cow? It was baffling, but if my husband was in as much trouble as he was telling me he was, then I needed to go all the way to the bottom of this and dig out the truth.

At least, that was how I was processing this in my mind.

CHAPTER 2

"Yes, herd," he repeated, stepping toward me. I should stop him, but I couldn't. Something about the word 'herd' weakened my knees, and I couldn't help but fall to the cement, the hard texture digging into the skin.

It was difficult to explain. There was this instant desire to submit myself to whatever he wanted to do, and that gleam in his eyes told me that he was aware of that, more so than he should be.

His buddies followed him slightly from behind, approaching me as well. One of them took some of my hair in his hand, sliding his fingers on it. I couldn't help but lock my eyes with his, wondering what was going on in his mind.

Glancing down, I noticed that he was sporting a huge boner, one that would wreck my throat, and I wasn't exaggerating. I was beginning to think that this might be the opportunity for me to rekindle the love for sex I didn't think I could have back, considering that John had never been good in bed.

He let go of my hair, letting his hand drop to his side. I thought that he wasn't going to do anything with it, but then he decided to surprise me. He lowered his pants, his dick jumping out and oozing his hunger for this.

The only thing that it wanted to do now was to wreck my throat.

Salivating, I didn't even know how I was going to externalize how much my body craved all of that, only knowing that it was going to happen one way or another.

After all, the way that I was kneeling on the ground told them as much.

Studying their faces, I could tell that they were slightly older than me, though that didn't mean much.

Jeremy stroked my chin with his hand, making me tilt my head up. "I think that there's something you want to do with us that you've been thinking about since seeing us, and now might be the right time to do something about that."

Swallowing the lump in my throat, I couldn't help but steal a glance at his bulge, imagining that I was going to suck him off right now and that nothing could be done to stop that.

After all, the moment he noticed that those thoughts were sprouting up in my mind, he turned me to the other side so that I was facing the guy whose dick was already pointing at me. He was the same one that had lowered his pants.

My goodness. His shaft was even bigger than I thought, and I couldn't even begin to guess how long it was. All I knew was that when it was entering my mouth, I wouldn't be able to do anything that wasn't gagging. And I wasn't exaggerating. I knew that was going to happen the moment that he locked his eyes with me. It was his way to inform me that this was starting now.

Stroking his big member, he said, "I think that we have something we should do first."

I remembered his name. It was Edward. A beautiful name. A name that I would never forget, too.

Right after that, he grabbed a handful of my hair and shoved my head down onto his prick, filling up my entire mouth. I couldn't think, and I couldn't properly process what was going on other than the fact that this was unbelievable.

Pleasure overflowing out of me, I could only rub and twist my nipples, wishing that something else was happening, but at the same time knowing that it couldn't.

After all, I had heard about the rumors floating around, rumors that talked about there being women who couldn't stop making milk, but I knew that they were all bullshit, and I should keep that in mind.

So much so that the only thing that I was focusing on was giving this man the best blowjob of his life, and it almost looked like it was working. After all, he was moaning and groaning loudly, this whole time guiding my head up and down on his prick, filling me up with everything he had, and it was a lot.

I couldn't even begin to describe it. I knew it was going to happen before it even started, and it was no surprise when my gag reflexes kicked in. My body wanted to take him out of me as much as it wanted him stuffing me even fuller than now, no matter how little sense that made.

At least, that was what I was telling myself, my climax coming and punching me through with it. It was the best thing that I thought was going to happen, and by the time it was over, I was huffing and groaning. I'd never thought, in my entire life, that breathing would become a difficult thing to do, but that was precisely what he was showing me now.

The moment I thought he was going to slip his dick out of me, he decided to surprise me by shoving it back all the way inside, and it punched into the back of my throat without a hint of mercy.

I didn't even know what was happening anymore, only that it was so good that he came inside of me, spewing out rope after rope of come in there, and it was sticky and warm.

I couldn't have enough of it, and that was putting it mildly.

My body was like a burning furnace, and I could only think about how much I wanted to have the other guys destroy me completely just like Edward did.

Edward chuckled, finally easing his prick out of my mouth. When he finished doing that, I found myself wishing to have him stuffing me again, and it was a pity that he was already putting his pants back on.

I knew that sometimes I could act like a slut, but I never thought that giving another man, who wasn't my husband, a blowjob in an underground parking lot was going to revive all those forbidden urges in me.

This was going to be the most memorable moment in my life, and I would never forget it.

CHAPTER 3

To be transformed into a hucow. Thinking about that, I couldn't help but realize that it all made sense, at least to me. Even my husband was supporting me with my decision, something that made me despise him even more.

And yet, now that I was again surrounded by the Dairy Club members, the only thing I could think about was that this was exactly what I needed. They were even already shirtless, just waiting for the right moment to strike, which was going to happen in a heartbeat.

"You just need to step into the chamber and it will change you."

I had even already seen one of the members of the Dairy Club that wasn't a man. At the moment, there were only four members in the organization, Jeremy included. The only female member was Stacy and she was so big. Her breasts hung low from her body, and she couldn't even walk around on her feet anymore, given her weight.

That was how much she had changed, and it was the same destiny that I wanted for myself.

So much so that I was already stepping into the chamber after giving my husband a look of disapproval. He failed me in so many ways it was impossible to account for all of them right now.

Despite that, he couldn't fight against his urge to give me to the Dairy Club. I accepted that, too. I accepted it all and it couldn't be any different. My pussy was already begging for all the pleasure that they were going to shower me with.

After a while, I noticed my body changing, but I didn't have enough time to witness everything and how it was changing me. I soon fell asleep and when I woke up, I was already outside of the chamber, the Dairy Club members surrounding me.

Just out in the distance was my husband, who was watching this from the best place he could be. It gave him the perfect view of this.

He couldn't even stop himself before sliding his hand under his pants, looking for only one thing, which was his dick. He began to pump it, the movement slow, feeling turned on by all this. I didn't even know how I managed to stay married to him this whole time. After all, he was no one more than my makeup artist, and I could even have already chosen someone else to replace him.

At least, that was what I was telling myself. One more thing that I noticed when I woke up was that I was naked from top to bottom. My body changed so much in such little time that it ripped the clothes off of me.

Now, I was exposed and the Dairy Club members could do anything to me, so much so that they were already salivating at the thought. Their plans for me were peppered with evilness.

"We've been waiting for this for such a long time," Jeremy murmured, taking my hand and helping me stand up. Without doing that, I wouldn't have been able to stand on my feet, which was a constant reminder about the changes in my body.

My mind was a little out of it and I wasn't thinking about anything in particular that didn't involve the members sucking me dry.

I knew they were even already thinking about doing that right now. No waiting; just going straight to what they yearned for.

His eyes checked me out from bottom to top, scrutinizing every part of me. I knew just how much he wanted all of that, and he wasn't the type of man to stop himself, especially when he could already see his goal.

Without giving it a second thought, he cupped my boob and brought the nipple into his mouth. I already knew that I was going to feel an insurmountable amount of pleasure when he did that, but I didn't think it was going to be so powerful, to the point where I thought I was going to come just from this alone.

A moment later, he began to apply pressure with his lips on my nipple, all the while his eyes remained locked with mine, and I didn't even know how to react to this. All I knew was that I had to come. Nothing else would do. So much so that my body was already beginning to tremble and I had to close my eyes, anticipating the moment I was going to reach my high.

But right when that was going to happen, I noticed someone positioning himself behind me, and upon peeking over my shoulder, I noticed that he was none other than Edward, the same man that had unloaded his milk into my mouth.

The parking lot. That's where it happened.

I was still thinking about that and how much I enjoyed everything. I swallowed all of his sperm and I would do it all again, no doubt about it.

He ran his finger up in my butt crack, enjoying the way that my body jerked as he finished doing that. I didn't know if I was supposed to feel pissed off or like what he just did. It was amazing, but it was also true that he ruined the moment I was going to climax.

That was everything I thought I wanted from this moment.

Upon noticing someone else approaching me, I gasped when I realized that he was Robert. He eased my other nipple between his lips and began to suckle out all the milk, not wasting a single drop.

Jesus.

I knew that all these guys were thirsty for my milk, but I didn't think that they were going to be milking me like this. My body couldn't keep up with all of this, especially now that Edward was behind me, fondling my butt cheeks.

If this continued without any changes, I would find myself on the verge of my high again and I would come much more strongly than it almost happened before.

I couldn't wait for that.

CHAPTER 4

Moaning. Groaning. Louder than ever before. I didn't even know what I was doing anymore, and I could still feel their hands roaming my entire body, looking for every possible way that they could please me.

Oh, God.

I was going to come.

I was going to reach my high and it was going to be devastating, so much so that I was already anticipating it all.

My body was burning.

My cells were on fire.

It was as though everything was moving in slow motion and faster than normal at the same time, and I couldn't even process what was going on.

All I knew was that it was good. Too good.

So much more than I thought it was going to be.

In a moment, I was trembling and coming, my orgasm sweeping through my body. My body still shaking, the only thing preventing me from falling to the floor was that Jeremy was still holding me.

He didn't want to let go of me at all.

Calming down, I reopened my eyes and locked them with his, wondering what was going to happen now. He retreated his head, faking that he was going to kiss me.

What a fucking bastard, I thought before recomposing myself the moment I noticed that Robert still had my other nipple inside his mouth, and I didn't think that he wanted to stop milking me. Not until he drank even the last drop, that was.

Not until I was dry to the point that my boob couldn't make any more milk in the next few hours.

"That was so good. I find it so arousing that your husband is watching everything and that he is enjoying it all," he commented, making me peer over his shoulder and find John splayed on the ground, cum covering his belly.

Jeremy probably didn't know that yet.

Damn. John just had the most rewarding orgasm of his life, but I didn't think it was so strong it blacked him out. I kind of wanted the same to happen to me.

But right now, I had to be worried about something else, or rather, someone else. Jeremy. He still had me pressed up against his body, his muscles against my curves. I could only wonder how I was going to feel when I was exploring every part of his body if he allowed me to do that.

"He is nobody to me," I said and Jeremy chuckled. While he did that, Edward slipped his finger into my butthole, gyrating inside of it. I couldn't help but groan and turn as much as I could, witnessing that wicked smile on his face.

I knew that he had something even eviler planned for me, but I didn't think that it was even worse than that.

"Why did you stop talking? Was it because of me?" He asked, his voice echoing in the basement. "Don't stop on my account. I was only enjoying the feeling of having my finger inside such a tight hole. There are so many things that I'm planning on doing to it."

He was still gyrating his finger in my butthole, making me moan and groan. But Jeremy didn't like that, and it was for that reason that he clamped his hand on my mouth, stopping me from continuing to do that.

I didn't know why he made me do that, but I supposed that he didn't want to think that one of his directors, who didn't hold a candle to him, was also showering me with pleasure. It was in every part of my body.

Something even more surprising was happening, I noticed the moment that milk drops started to seep out of my nipples again. I couldn't help but be surprised by the occurrence, imagining that, this whole time, I couldn't make more of that in the next few hours at least.

Right after that, Robert slipped my teat into his mouth, suckling on it for what was already feeling like an eternity.

He knew what he was doing, his hands massaging and fondling my boob. He hit every right spot doing that, and his movements combined with Edward's expert finger sliding and rubbing in my hole brought me closer to my climax, and it was going to burst whether Jeremy wanted it or not.

They were all around me, not giving me any space. I couldn't even breathe properly, and I feared that I was going to suffocate.

Thankfully, I knew that Jeremy would stop that before it happened. After all, I was one of the most important assets in the Dairy Club and he couldn't risk something like that materializing.

Groaning and mooing, I thought that those things were going to happen, but then Jeremy yanked me out of there, and I fell on my ass on the floor in the basement. Snapping my head up, I couldn't help but ask why he did that. It didn't make much sense unless he had something else planned for me.

"I think it's about time we taught you some manners, Sheryl."

I didn't even know what he meant by that, but the possibilities behind his words piqued my interest, and I couldn't help but wonder what it all meant.

How was he going to 'teach me some manners?'

CHAPTER 5

"Uhh, what?" I asked, still wondering what he meant by that.

"You need to be branded," he explained and the thought made me smile even though I shouldn't.

They were going to brand me? Every time I went outside, everyone would know I was theirs. I wasn't going to become a full-fledged member of the Dairy Club. I was going to be like their trophy, and they would be able to show me off to everyone.

Just the possibility of that happening was enticing me, making me salivate.

Edward chuckled. "We knew that you were going to enjoy the thought so much that the only thing you can think about right now is how rewarding it will be when it's all happening."

"Yes, Master, that's exactly what I need and want," I said and he went to the other side of the basement, heating up a rod and then coming back with it, holding it with only one hand. The rod was heavy, but only one of his arms was sufficient to hold it.

Glancing to do right, I noticed that my husband was still sleeping on the floor, passed out. I didn't think that he would wake up anytime soon.

In the end, I found my true calling, and I couldn't see myself moving out of here anytime soon.

Now that Edward was back with the rod in his hand, he wasted no time before pressing on the right buttcheek. From this moment onward, every time someone looked at it, they would know I was theirs and theirs alone.

I couldn't be shared with anyone else, so much so that I knew I was going to have to drop my job as an actress. My career was over, but it wasn't sad. If anything, it was what I had always wanted, even though I didn't know that until now.

It hurt. I wasn't going to deny it, but it still felt right. I even lifted my butt, showing them that they could eat my ass now if they so wished.

They wouldn't be taking my virginity – after all, John was the one who did it – but it would still be like that. They knew I was tight and begging for them to impale me with their thick, swollen poles.

I was already getting obsessed over the thought of that happening.

"And now, I'm going to collar you," Robert murmured before producing a collar and putting it around my neck. His hand was holding the leash and he could take me now wherever he wanted.

With his eyes telling me that he was going to do that, we went up the stairs to the first floor of the house. It was more like an estate than a house, and I couldn't help but want to explore everything.

The collar and the leash tugged slightly, indicating to me where he wanted to take me.

The estate had some workers and they witnessed me going everywhere with them. I couldn't deny that crawling about like this was difficult. I was still getting used to it, but it was as though I was finding my calling.

My body was trembling.

My knees and hands hurt feeling the cement and the grass, but few things in life were better than bathing in the sunlight, naked and exposed. It was much better than spending any amount of time in that sex dungeon, even though it was also where we had everything we needed.

After walking with me for a little while, we stopped, and then he indicated that we were going back inside the house again. I groaned thinking about that. If there was something I wanted, it was them fucking me outside and where everybody could see us.

Some employees would even record us, which was one of the reasons why I wanted to make that happen.

My boobs swung heavily under me, but despite their weight, I wasn't thinking about them much. I knew that soon I would even stop noticing that they were so much different now.

We entered another room in the house. It was as dark as the sex dungeon, but something was in the middle of it. I had never seen such a contraption, and I had no idea what it did.

All I knew was that it fit an entire human in it in a lying position.

A slap hit my butt, making me turn my head up and find Jeremy beaming at me.

"That's what we call a milking machine and it will milk you until there is really nothing left in you. We aren't planning on selling your milk to anyone, but we will store it and then we will have some jugs to drink from. After all, we heard that milk from pretty girls like you can make our muscles look even better than they already are, and we want to get bigger than this."

His muscles would grow bigger? He would have to buy new clothes, then!

I supposed that soon we would find out if he was right, considering that he already chugged down a lot of my milk. And that was without mentioning Stacy, too.

I couldn't help but wait to see if it was true or not.

Just after that, they eased me into the machine and connected the suction cups to my udders. Waiting for the process to start, I gasped when I realized that Edward was already positioning himself behind me.

He was going to fuck me without discussing with the other guys who should go first?

Damn. I knew that he was cocky, but not to the point where he thought he could go up against those guys.

I never thought that he was going to slide his prick inside of me first. I had already basked in his sperm filling up my mouth, and now he was going to reward me by doing the same in my cunt.

I couldn't wait until that happened, so much so that I gasped when he slid his prick inside of me with little to no resistance. I knew that he was going to fuck me from behind without any warning, but I didn't think that he could ease his dong inside of me in one fell swoop. No difficulty at all when doing that…

I didn't even have time to react before he was already pounding in and out of me.

CHAPTER 6

Still doing that, I wasn't surprised when Robert came over holding something in his hand. It was a ball gag, and even though I didn't want it, there was no denying that right now he was going to do whatever he pleased.

"Open your mouth," he commanded and I could do only that. A moment later, I pressed my teeth into the ball gag, hoping that I could burst it by doing that, but I realized how stupid I was being, so I stopped it.

It just wasn't going to happen.

So, I was branded, collared, and now he was pistoning in and out of me, destroying me from the inside out. The good thing about this was that I was making even more milk than before, the liquid gushing out into the suction cups. I could feel them applying pressure and milking everything I had, not leaving anything.

In the meantime, the other guys were only watching, and I wondered what they were going to do. They were going to do something, right?

I didn't have to ask myself that much, considering that Jeremy was already coming forward. What was he going to do? I asked myself. Since I was gagged, there was no way that he could fuck my mouth, no matter how much I wanted him to do that.

Just when I was still asking myself that question, Edward erupted inside of me, shooting rope after rope of milk inside of me. I was certain that he was getting me pregnant by doing that, but I didn't say anything about it.

Huffing and groaning, I could only wonder what else was going to happen next the moment he jammed his prick into me one final time, claiming me as his.

Panting, I didn't think that I could go for another round, even though my body begged me to do that. It didn't know its own limits.

Jeremy smiled, walking until he stood behind me, and then he eased his dong into my cunt. I didn't even have time to think about what was happening, and I hated that I couldn't say anything thanks to the gag in my mouth.

Why did they have to gag me?

Oh, I knew why.

They needed to feel that they had full control over me, which was working.

In more ways than I thought possible.

Jeremy was the kind of guy that needed even more control than that, so he wasted no time before grabbing the end of the leash and tugging it until my neck bent. I thought that he was going to keep bending it until it broke, but he didn't.

Thank goodness. I couldn't do much more, the ball gag stifling all the sounds coming out of my mouth. We should have decided on a gesture that allowed me to stop this anytime I wanted to.

He was holding and tugging the leash to bring me slightly closer to him, and also to ascertain that I knew he was the one in control.

The older man pounded in and out of me like a savage beast, his balls slapping against my ass. Moaning and groaning against the ball gag, I didn't even know if this time I was going to stay awake.

I felt that my body was going to give up and I was going to pass out.

It wouldn't be the first time that happened.

The most interesting thing about this was that John wasn't even around. Still passed out on the floor, most likely dreaming that he was a better and bigger man than these billionaires.

That was hilarious.

"Fuck. You were so fucking tight," Jeremy groaned before erupting inside of me. His dick slapped and throbbed in my cunt, shooting out rope after rope of his come, and I could only continue to moo even with the ball gag in my mouth.

It didn't matter. It wasn't going to stop me from enjoying this as much as I could.

By the time it was all over, I could only hope that they were already tired of me and were going to leave me alone, even though I didn't think that they were going to do that. Not yet, anyway.

I was certain of that because there was still Robert's turn and I knew he was hungry for it. So much so that he locked his eyes with Jeremy's and the latter stepped away from me after shooting one last rope of his milk in my cunt.

Now that they were knocking me up, I wasn't going to know who the father of the baby was going to be. I could even have multiple babies at the same time, a thought that filled me with joy.

Sliding his hand down my spine, he positioned himself behind me and then infiltrated my cunt with his dong, taking his time.

Huffing, I was sweating and my eyes kept on closing. I had to keep fighting against the need to fall asleep. No matter how much part of my body wanted that, it wasn't going to happen.

I took a deep breath the moment Robert filled me with his dong, going all the way. I couldn't deny that my pussy was sore, more so than it had ever been before in my life, and after this, I knew that I would never be the same again.

"I'm going to fuck you until you black out," he promised – or maybe it was more like a threat – and then he began to do exactly that. He didn't exaggerate whatsoever.

By the time he picked up the pace and his balls were slapping on my ass, I blacked out.

When I woke up, I had no idea what would happen.

EPILOGUE

Waking up, I found a familiar figure sitting by my side. She was knitting something, making me wonder what it was. And more than that, she made me wonder why she was here instead of offering her ass for those billionaires. I was pretty certain that Jeremy and his buddies were already obsessing over the possibility of fucking her, especially now that she was pregnant and couldn't get pregnant twice in a row.

It wasn't that they worried about that. It just made them feel freer and nothing more than that.

"I'm sorry, Stacy, but what do you think you're doing here?" I asked. She was supposed to be elsewhere on the property, getting ready to let the billionaires take her any way they wanted.

At least, that was how it was supposed to be, I remembered.

"I'm knitting something for you," she explained as if it was the most basic thing she ever said in her life, and considering that she was turning into a bimbo, it could be.

"But why?" I asked. Curiosity took hold of me. We already knew each other, but I didn't think that she liked me so much – not to the point of knitting a gift for me.

"You are pregnant," she revealed, lifting her head and beaming at me.

I widened my eyes, even though it was no surprise. I had to fake it. Something I was learning about living here was that the billionaires wanted to live in a dream where everybody was always happy and smiling.

"Oh, really?" I asked even though I didn't want to know the answer.

"Yeah. That's what the doctor told me, at least," she said and then lifted the thing that she was creating. It was a small onesie, made of yarn.

I wasn't going to deny that it was kind of cute.

I had just about enough strength to hold the small onesie in my hand, too. That sex burned all the energy I had, to the point that I passed out. I couldn't remember what happened since then, having shown up here.

Doing that, I reflected on everything that happened before this moment. I reflected on the billionaires knocking me up and freeing me from John.

Remembering him, though, I couldn't help but wonder where he was and what he was doing.

Speak of the devil, I thought the moment he showed up at the door, but he wasn't standing. In fact, he was on all fours and wore a mask. A mask of a dog. I had to hold back the chuckle that formed in my throat.

I had always known that he was a cuck, but I never thought that it was so deeply rooted in him. I mean, he couldn't even look at himself in a mirror anymore and still recognize the person he had once been.

Or that I'd thought he'd once been. He was a spineless idiot who shouldn't even be a man.

And I knew that I could humiliate him even more, especially with that collar and the leash that Jeremy was holding.

From this moment onward, he was our official cuck.

BOSSY HUCOW MÉNAGE

CHAPTER 1

I felt like I was trapped. Trapped with this guy, who didn't know what to do with me. We were sitting on the couch, watching something on TV. What were we watching? I couldn't even pay attention to what the screen was displaying.

And despite him making me think that I was wasting my time, I couldn't help but sneak my hand under his pants and look for his cock.

"Warren, you are my boyfriend, so you better make me think that this is worth it."

He turned his head to look at me and there was something different in his eyes. Even though what I had just said was a little more direct than what I usually said when we were having some sexy time, he still didn't try to rebuke me.

For now, he was just looking at me and probably thinking about how pitiful he was. I would never hide that about him. He was like that and there wasn't much he could do about it other than feel humiliated.

At least his cock was a little bit bigger than the average size, but it was still not enough for me. Every time that I thought about it, I found myself wanting a massive, oversized prick to grip with my hand. And I could already imagine myself sliding my hand on it, devouring it.

Would that ever happen? I didn't think so. I wasn't holding my breath for it.

"Sorry, love. It's just the way I am and I think that you should have known that things are this way with me. If anything, you should be more open-minded about who I am."

I groaned, putting my hand around his cock and beginning to stroke it. We were alone in my room, but I was wishing we were in a public space, like a subway car so that everybody could see how slutty I was. I was like that and I didn't hide that from anybody.

"You're making me so disappointed in being your girlfriend, and that's something I thought I would never say," I said before increasing the speed of my hand and now it was going up and down, making Warren even harder than he was already. He had thought that was impossible, I could tell just by looking at his eyes.

Then, I glanced down, finding his prick, which was already outside of his pants. After that, I began to fondle his balls, and I could tell that he was already on the verge of having a climax.

When it happened, it would wash over his entire body and he would most likely pass out, just like it happened so many times when I thought we were going to have sex.

Another reason why I thought he was a puny, worthless man was the fact that he didn't want to fuck me properly and take my virginity.

My pussy was begging for a proper man to do that and I could only wonder when the right opportunity to accomplish that was going to present itself.

A few seconds after that and Warren exploded in my hand, shooting out rope after rope of his come all over his belly, which was another reason why this was disappointing.

I wanted him doing this either in my mouth or in my pussy. I wanted him splitting me open and cumming in there, breeding me with his heir.

My mouth was already salivating just thinking about that.

Alas, it wasn't going to happen – at least, not tonight. After he finished cumming on my hand, he shut his eyes and didn't open them again. And he was even already snoring and showing me that he wasn't interested in anything else tonight.

All in all, this was as disappointing as I thought it was going to be and one of the reasons why we had to break up right now.

I kissed him on his cheek and said, "Warren, I think that I'm going to break up with you. My life is boring enough working as a secretary for those millionaires, and I think that I want to take Mr. Leach up on his offer. I want him to turn me into a hucow and you are okay with that, right?"

I checked his eyes and… Yeah. I knew that he didn't have anything to say about that and even though he would miss me a lot after finding out that I was now living there with them, he could shove his worry about me up his ass.

Anyway, now I had to wipe my hand and clean it. I did that and then I took off my clothes, going to the bathroom. I needed to take a shower.

After doing that, I imagined Jeremy exploring my body with his hands, feeling every part of me. I imagined him stuffing me full with his dick and breeding me with his heir. And while doing that, I couldn't hold back the climax that surged in me, and it was devastating in a way that I never thought possible.

My body was even shaking and trembling, something that Warren could never replicate with me. That was how powerful my crush on Jeremy was.

Mr. Bleach. I imagined myself saying his name loudly while riding on his prick until he filled me with his thick, viscous cum.

My body was still feeling the aftershocks of that amazing orgasm, and that wasn't something that happened often. That was just how strong my need for Jeremy was.

Alright, it was decided. Tonight. No, *right now* I was going to call him and tell him the good news. Then, perhaps he would come to pick me up right here in my house instead of making me wait.

I never liked waiting.

CHAPTER 2

But he was making me wait. I was outside of my home and Warren was doing everything in his power to make me change my mind, but it wasn't going to work like that.

I pushed him away from me with my hand. "Warren, no matter how much you insist, I'm not going to change my mind. I'm going to the Dairy Club and I'm going to become their hucow. If you want, you can watch us as we have fun, but other than that, there isn't much you can do."

His eyes were still wide and he blinked several times in a row as if he was trying to understand what I said. After he realized that he was only wasting his time right now, he straightened up his spine and said, "alright, then I'm going with you, but only to make sure..."

"You want to be sure about what?" I asked, curious about what he was thinking. What was he thinking was going to happen when we were having fun and Jeremy was pounding in and out of me without mercy?

He was crazy if he was thinking that he could stop me from cheating on him. To be honest, I was only asking myself why it took me so long to make this decision.

A few seconds later, when Warren was opening his mouth again to ask me whatever else he thought he still needed to ask me, a limousine pulled over in front of me, and I knew that was Jeremy.

His window rolled down, revealing him. I opened a big smile

and the driver opened the door for me. I found myself with Jeremy sitting by my side. After Warren tried to get into the limousine, Jeremy put his hand against his chest, stopping him.

"I don't know what you think you're doing, but you are not allowed inside. Diana told me everything about what was going on with you and she doesn't want to be with you anymore. It's as simple as that."

Warren opened his mouth and for a moment I really thought that he was going to grow a pair, but then he shook his head and started to walk away.

I decided that I wasn't going to waste the opportunity to make him see everything, so I grabbed his hand and made him fall onto the seat, sitting by my other side.

Jeremy couldn't help but widen his eyes, asking me what I thought I was doing. "Trust me on this. With Warren around, the humiliation will be even more tempting and delicious. My pussy is already wet just thinking about it."

He licked his lips. "Your pussy is already like that? Wanna show me?" He asked, his eyes flashing with evilness.

I lowered my hand and put it under my pair of pants, dipping it into the wetness between my legs. Then, I took it out of there and showed it to him, nearing it to his nose.

He lowered his head, taking a good, long whiff. Then, he smirked, saying, "Ohh, Jesus. After smelling it, I feel like devouring you right now. I feel like I shouldn't even wait until Robert is with us. You really know how to tempt a man like me."

I smiled, looking at Warren, who couldn't stop blinking. What was he so surprised about?

I couldn't care less about what he was thinking right now, so I just decided to ignore him for the time being. I was also wet for something else, that being Jeremy's monster cock, and I was thinking that I couldn't wait until we were in his estate to have a little fun.

It was for that reason that I put my hand on his bulge and began to massage it, applying pressure on it at regular intervals. His eyes flashed with evilness again and he breathed heavily, putting his hand under my boob.

I could feel his hand applying pressure on it slowly and carefully. He knew what he was doing, and that wasn't surprising.

I moaned and put my fingers around his cock, stroking it, all the while relishing the fact that this was all happening while my former boyfriend could see every detail. And he was still so dumbfounded by all this that he couldn't do anything.

He couldn't fight back.

And just like so many times before this, I ignored him, letting out another moan of pleasure through my lips the moment I knew my orgasm was coming, and it was even better than I thought, one of the reasons why I sped up my hand, shooting it up and down his prick.

He was going to make me come as much as I was going to do the same to him.

By now, the limousine was already driving and I knew that we didn't have much time until we reached his estate. When we got there, Robert would surely smell that something happened, but he wouldn't be able to do anything.

And that was another reason why this spiced things up, my breathing accelerating. And then, it happened, my body trembling while he still fondled and massaged my boobs. I swear, it was as if he couldn't stop this even if he wanted to.

A moment after that, Jeremy exploded in my hand and coated it with his milk, making it wet. It was just as I thought it was going to be. It was mind-shattering and even after it was over, I could still feel the aftershocks of the amazing orgasm that he rewarded me with, and even though I couldn't know this for sure, I could still see that he thought the same way.

He moved his hand off my boob, saying, "that was amazing and I want to do it again with you. I want to do it after you've transformed. I feel that, after that, it will be even more rewarding than it was tonight, don't you think?"

And after he asked me that, I could only wonder if what he was proposing was going to happen tonight as well.

I couldn't help but hope that that was exactly what was going to happen.

CHAPTER 3

I opened my eyes and found myself lying on the bed, wondering where Jeremy was. He said that as soon as the transformation was over, he was going to be by my side and give me a lot of pleasure.

I licked my lips, thinking about that. Was it going to take him too long to show up?

The room was dark and I couldn't see much. This was so infuriating, I thought after some seconds filled with waiting and more of the same. Even though I couldn't say this for sure, I was beginning to think that he fooled me when he said that he was going to be around here waiting for my transformation to finish.

And it did finish. I didn't need to look at myself in the mirror to know that.

I stood up and began to walk around the room, looking for the light switch, and struggling with doing that. I didn't know what was going on, but it felt like the switch was nowhere to be found, which was annoying.

"Dammit, where the fuck is it?" I asked myself, in a moment feeling a hand landing on my shoulder and, after gasping, I realized that the person behind me was none other than… Robert! I hadn't seen him after coming here, and this entire time I had been asking myself where he was.

"Robert?" I asked. I had seen his face before, so I recognized it immediately after seeing him.

The most surprising thing about this was that he had been

in the same room with me the entire time. One other surprising thing about this was that he was naked from top to bottom, and his body was even more delicious than Jeremy's.

To be honest, fuck Jeremy. He made me wait this entire time to see if he was going to come and fuck me, and now I was with someone that was going to fill in the gap left by him.

"That's right, pretty. It's me."

"Have you been watching me sleep this entire time?" I asked. I had to go straight to the point with that, and he wasn't fazed by my question.

"No, of course not," he gave me a devilish smile. "I would never do something like that. In fact, I was only waiting for you to wake up. I want to fuck you right now and I think that you want the same, don't you?"

Right after saying that, he put his fingers around his dick, and I couldn't help but wonder if he was even bigger than Jeremy.

I also couldn't stop licking my lips, and I supposed that was something that was going to be happening a lot more often from now on.

"Everything you want to do to me, Master. I want you to fuck me, but there is a condition."

"Oh, there is? You are feeling pretty bossy right now, aren't you?"

He began to pump his shaft slowly, enticing me to go down on my knees in front of him and suck him off. To be honest, I was only wondering when he was going to ask me to do that. My mind was already obsessing over the idea of making that real.

To feel his massive dong filling my mouth with everything that he had, and then he would even feed me with his semen. I just felt overwhelmed by the possibility of that happening.

"Yeah, there's that condition and I think that you should respect it."

He guffawed.

"You really are different from the other members we have here, which is one of the reasons why I think that we are going to get along just fine." I opened my mouth, but then he added, "and

I think that we should go where I can brand you. Don't worry, it won't take long. Jeremy has already left the rod heated, after all."

He was really going to brand me? It wasn't enough that I was transformed into his hucow, he was also going to make sure that anybody else that saw me knew that I was his. Theirs. A member of the Dairy Club.

I already felt shivers running down my spine just hearing that.

He took me outside of his house and then he brought the heated rod, asking me to go down on all fours, which I did. Following that, he pressed the end of the heated rod to my butt, which was the region where everybody could see the mark. It was a welt that could never be removed and that thought already made the hair on my skin shoot up.

I was his and nothing and no one would change that, I thought with a smile on my face. After that, he went behind me and settled his hands on my ass, kneeling behind me. I couldn't help but wonder what he was going to do, and I was nicely surprised when he began to massage it.

After a while, I started to wish he was fondling my boobs. They were already aching to be milked, one of the reasons why they were already leaking.

And as if he could read my mind, Robert leaned over, putting his mouth close to my ear. "Don't worry, pretty. I'm going to milk you when the time is right. For now, I'm preparing you for something naughty that I'm planning on doing to you."

Something naughty that he was planning to do to me? I couldn't help but wonder what that was, but I didn't have much time to think about that, considering that he just took something in his hand, and then, without any other preparation, he slid something into my ass.

And I had to wonder what it was.

CHAPTER 4

Robert slid his hand over the back of my neck, saying, "it's a butt plug, silly. What did you think it was?"

I moaned and... mooed. That was right. I mooed and it felt right to do that. In fact, I could do so much more since I was beginning to feel less like the person I was and much more like the hucow that he showed me I was.

He moved his hands around me and he found my boobs, massaging and fondling them for what felt like an eternity. With his body on top of mine, I could only wonder how much longer I was going to last until I came. After all, my body was already growing warmer and sweat drops were forming on the skin, and I could feel my climax growing in intensity.

Robert continued to knead my breasts for a couple more minutes before moving his hands away, and it happened the moment that I thought I was going to come. Turning my head to look over my shoulder, I asked, "why did you do that? It's so unfair."

"Because, right now, I want to milk you and I don't want you to come so quickly without us first doing something special," he responded and then kissed the nape of my neck, sending shockwaves of pleasure through me.

I even arched my back, something that never happened every time Warren did this to me.

And I couldn't help but wonder where he was.

A few seconds after that, we heard footsteps walking into the room. I turned my head to see who it was and I was hoping that it was Jeremy, but it turned out that he was just Warren.

My pathetic ex. He didn't have anything else to do with me other than how much he wanted to see a better man using me, and he was getting his wish right now.

I chuckled.

What else was I going to do when my ex decided to show up and prove that, in the end, he really was nothing more than an asshole that never deserved me?

"Warren? What do you think you are doing here?" I asked, going straight to the point.

"I was just... Checking to see if you needed anything."

I cackled. I couldn't believe that he came here just to see if I needed something, one of the reasons why I found him to be so pathetic.

Robert looked up and found him. "If you are so intent on helping us, then you can help us by cleaning her milk on the floor."

Warren blinked twice in a row. "You want me to... clean her milk on the floor? But I don't even have a piece of cloth and a floor squeegee."

Robert waved his hand, showing annoyance. "You aren't going to need those things. You can do it with your tongue and lips."

Warren opened and closed his mouth several times in a row and he truly couldn't understand what he should do. The moment that Robert showed he was going to punish him for being so clueless, he rushed to me and positioned himself underneath me.

I knew that he could move fast when he wanted to, but I didn't think that he could humiliate himself even more than he had done several times before in his life.

He met my eyes one more time before putting his tongue out and beginning to lick the milk on the floor. It was already leaking, so there was a sizable pool on the floor.

Despite his thirst, it was still going to take him a while to lick everything off the floor. And for a moment, I couldn't do anything but watch my ex underneath me, his tongue sweeping over the milk pool.

After chuckling again, Robert prodded my pussy with his prick, trying to slide it in. I looked over my shoulder and asked him if he was going to do that right now, and he confirmed it by just easing his dong inside of me, one inch at a time.

Grimacing, I didn't think that it was going to be so painful, to the point where I thought my sex would never be the same after this.

"Oh God, oh God," I mumbled over and over again, and at that moment I had already forgotten that Warren was still licking the milk on the floor.

Was he doing a good job? I didn't know. I couldn't even hear the noise that his tongue was making, swiping on the liquid.

After a while, Robert managed to put himself all the way inside of me, and then he stopped. He didn't do anything, which made me wonder what his plans were now.

"Jesus. It's really so big. I never thought that there was a man so big in the world," I confessed after huffing. Breathing was so difficult now, but it was nothing to worry about.

After looking down, I saw that my ex had almost finished licking the milk on the floor. There wasn't much more left of it on the floorboards, and even though my udders were still leaking more of it, it would take a while until there was another sizable pool on the floor.

"And, right now, I'm going to eat your pussy and take your virginity. You want me to do that, don't you?"

I smiled and confirmed, "it's everything I want, actually. I want you to do that and to show my ex that he could never be the same man you are."

"That I can do," he confirmed before rolling his hips, slowly in the beginning but then picking up the pace a couple of seconds later when he was used to what he was doing. In a few seconds after that, he was doing it at full speed, destroying my sex while slapping his balls against my ass.

We could all hear the slapping sounds echoing in the room and it only added to the feeling that this was the best sex dungeon that ever existed in the world.

I moaned, groaned, and mooed, all the while wondering when he was going to come into my sex. I was fertile and he could get me pregnant by doing this. I was sure that was one of his plans, even.

CHAPTER 5

A few seconds after that, I couldn't hold back the rising orgasm in me, and it was devastating when it happened.

My body shook with everything it had and I thought that I would never recover from such a powerful, shattering experience, one of the reasons why I was hoping that this was going to be it for today and we could relax until we had more energy for another round.

But I didn't know if that was what Robert had in mind, and I wasn't going to risk asking. I wasn't that crazy. The last thing that I wanted to do was to piss him off.

A few seconds after that, I looked down and saw Warren looking back up at me, smiling with some of my milk still on his lips.

He just looked so pathetic it made me wonder how I was able to put up with him for so long.

I moved my hand around his face, saying, "you did a good job cleaning up, but now... Scram. Get out. I don't want to see you around here right now."

He opened his mouth and he was going to say something, but then I put my index finger on it and stopped him. Whatever he had to say to me, I didn't want to hear it.

He stood up in a heartbeat and then disappeared from the room, leaving me alone with Robert, who guffawed.

"You really put him back in his place. That was amazing and funny at the same time," he said before erupting inside of me, shooting rope after rope of his come and filling me up with it. And there was so much of it that some was even dripping out and staining the floor again.

It was a reason to think that maybe I was a little too hasty when I ordered him to go out. He could do another cleanup job, this time focusing on the come that was now pooling on the floor.

But that was something for another time and, right now, I was focusing on gripping Robert's dong inside of me, and it was… Breathtaking.

He stretched my walls to the point that I was certain they would never be the same ever again. I couldn't help but wonder when the baby bump would become noticeable.

But as with so many other things, that was something for another time, and I could only focus on feeling Robert's massive dick inside of me. It almost felt like he wasn't thinking about pulling out anytime soon.

"This is so good," he purred before sliding his hand over my shoulders, focusing on all the pressure points. It was as if he was massaging them.

"I think that you shouldn't pull out. I want you inside of me for the rest of my life," I pleaded, smiling.

But in the meantime, I couldn't help but wonder when he was going to fuck my asshole, too. In fact, my mind was already obsessed over that, one of the reasons why I wanted it to happen right at this moment.

Sometimes, I could be impatient, just like it was happening now.

"Really? That would be so unfair to Jeremy. I'm pretty sure that he is already coming here, after all, and we don't want to disappoint him. He is as entitled to you as I am."

"You're right, but it would be so unfair to me if you pulled out right now. That's why I'm hoping you aren't going to do it. Or, if you do it, I hope that you do it slowly. I don't want it to happen so fast. After all, I'm still getting used to feeling you inside of me, and I'm certain you can understand me."

"I understand you, pretty," he said before gliding over my ass, following its curvature. I wanted him to finger me, but the butt plug was still in there. By now, enough time had already passed to the point that I couldn't even fill it inside of me anymore. It was as if it had always been a part of me. "But Jeremy and I are buddies, and I would never cross him."

I groaned, but couldn't argue. Robert was right about that even if I didn't want to admit it.

A few minutes after that, he began to pull out of me, and he did it quickly, much to my disappointment. Wondering what was going to happen next, I was happily surprised when Jeremy showed up at the door.

Now that I was thinking about it and this thought was popping into my mind, I wondered if Warren could show up here again so that he could finish another cleanup job after these millionaires were done with me.

He was already naked, as he should be. He was ready to get into the fun with Robert, who had already finished pulling out of me, his semen dripping from the slit. Just looking at it, I felt a sliver of thirst in me.

But my attention was quickly returned to the man standing in the doorway, who was already pumping his dick and preparing for this inevitable moment.

"I'm going to fuck you so hard in the ass right now and by the time I'm done with you, you will be begging for more and more. If there is something that all the other members of the Dairy Club think I am, it's how ruthless I can be when I'm in the right mood."

I licked my lips. If he was going to be so ruthless when fucking my ass, then I was already waiting for that to happen.

My body was even begging for that.

CHAPTER 6

It was only a few seconds after that that he went behind me, filling in the gap left by his buddy. I knew that he was going to do that, but I was still surprised by it and for a moment I didn't know how to react.

But the moment that he put his fingers around the loop on the butthole, I knew exactly what to do, and I mooed.

He slid his hand over my shoulder, enjoying the softness of my skin.

"Are you ready for this?" He asked, tugging at the butthole, but without removing it. Not yet, anyway. He was taking his time and, in the meantime, Robert positioned himself in front of me, teasing me with his prick. Licking my lips, I thought about sucking him off right now but only with his permission.

"I am," I responded without having to think too much about it. It was just the right thing to say at the moment, and it put me even more into the right mood than I already was, and I could just imagine him now filling me with his dong.

After that happened, he would shower me with even more pleasure than I could endure, and I wasn't kidding.

"Good. That's exactly the answer I was looking for," he murmured into my ear before pulling the buttplug out one inch at a time. He was taking his time doing that and I loved that about him, one of the reasons why I wanted him stuffing me full with his massive, oversized dong.

And to think that it was going to happen now... I just couldn't wait any longer.

A few seconds after that, the butt plug was out of my asshole. It had come out with an audible pop. I could already feel my walls trying to return to how they were, but they couldn't.

My asshole would never be the same and I wasn't exaggerating.

He slid his finger around my asshole, feeling the ridges. "Jesus, it's really something else, just like Robert here said it was, and I can't wait until I'm inside of it. Fucking an asshole is so much better than eating a pussy, not to mention that Robert was already the first inside of you there, so I want to do something a little bit more different."

I knew what he meant by that and I could only moo when he slid his finger into my hole, widening it a little bit more by pressing his fingers against the walls. I knew he was going to do that, but it still kind of caught me by surprise. I had really thought that he was going to plunge deep inside of me with his shaft.

I was already pleading for that to happen.

I mooed again and he said, "it's so warm and still tight. I'm pretty sure that when I'm inside of you, you will feel more pain than you think possible, and that's putting it mildly."

I knew he was right about that, and my expectations for that inevitable moment were only increasing right now.

Robert, after teasing me that he was going to let me suck him off, slid under me, grabbing both of my boobs. With his hands already massaging and kneading the skin, it took him very little time to show me exactly what he was going to do, and I could only groan when he eased one of my nipples into his hungry mouth.

He slid his tongue around it and continued to do what he was doing for what felt like an eternity, and then he began to suckle on it, drawing out milk. That continued to happen while Jeremy only teased that he was going to eat my rectum, and I could only hope that he wasn't going to take much longer to do that.

A few seconds after that, Jeremy eased his prick inside of me, one inch at a time and I could only curl my toes. The pain was almost intolerable, but I didn't say anything and just decided to bite my bottom lip as much as I could without drawing out blood. I felt that, if that happened, I would be more worried about what was happening to me than I already was.

A few seconds after that, Jeremy was already fully inside of me and I could even feel his balls pressing against my ass. I was still getting used to his size the moment that he started to pound in and out of me, and the most surprising thing about this was that he was at top speed from the get-go.

Moaning and groaning, I could only shut my eyes right now. The best thing about this was that they were both pleasing me from both ends, and they were relentless.

The only thing I did that I thought I wasn't going to was to look to the left when I heard footsteps coming from the door. It was, just like I had thought it was, Warren and he was even already jacking off while watching this development.

It really turned him on, didn't it?

A few moments after that, my body began to shake and I erupted. I was having the best orgasm of my life, and I wasn't exaggerating. A few moments after that, Jeremy erupted inside of me, and even though he wasn't going to knock me up just like his friend did, it was still a moment I would never forget.

I was huffing by the time this was over and he remained inside of me even after he spurted out the last rope of come. In the meantime, Robert emptied my jugs, and I knew that it was going to take a lot of time before they were filled with milk again.

This was such a memorable moment that I didn't want both of them to stop what they were doing. And as if he could read my mind, Jeremy confirmed as he murmured into my ear, "don't worry, pretty. We still have so much energy to burn and we are going to do that with you. We are going to come into your pussy and all your holes several more times, and then we'll show everyone that you are ours."

EPILOGUE

A few moments after that, it was determined that nobody else could enter the Dairy Club. It was an exclusive club that wasn't accepting any more members, and it only filled me with joy that I was one of the few women allowed to be a part of it.

In the meantime, Warren became my servant, and now he had to do everything I wanted. He even had to wear a puppy mask and a tail, all to please me. He had always been a puppy to me, but now it was official and he had to play by my rules even more than before.

That was one of the reasons why I put my legs over his body. He was on all fours before me and I was sitting on the couch. While doing that, I brought up the grape cluster I was holding in my hand, and then I popped one of the grapes into my mouth, savoring it.

"Hmm," I said, enjoying this a lot more than I thought I was going to.

Right after that, Warren said, "I'm so happy that you are enjoying yourself a lot more with those guys. I'm nothing like that, and that's something that I've already grown used to. It's okay, really. Sometimes, a man just has to realize that he is inferior."

I cackled and, while putting another grape into my mouth, I heard footsteps coming into the room and I turned my head to see who it was. I wasn't surprised when I found none other than Jeremy, Robert, and the other members of the club with them.

They were all here, including the other hucows. They were all gazing at my glistening pussy, and I knew that they wanted to do unforgivable things to it, things that we would never be able to erase.

Stacy and Sheryl… They were kind of jealous of me, but they had been in the same situation before, and they knew what it was like to be pampered by these millionaires.

As usual, every time that they were here, they were naked and their shafts were pointing at me. Glancing at them, I licked my lips. I wanted to mouth them for hours on end, and that just might happen now.

"Are you ready for this, Diana?" Jeremy asked, his eyes flashing with evilness. "When we start round two with you, we will pound you until there's nothing left of you, and by the time that we are done, you will be begging for more of it and we will claim you so hard that it will be impossible for you to remain awake. You will most likely pass out and you are okay with that, aren't you?"

And after hearing his words, I could only nod.

Of course I had no problems with that.

The End

If you want more books like this one, check these out:

1. Milked by Miners
2. Milked by the Irish Mafia
3. Shameless Bimbos
4. Creamy Harem
5. Holiday Milking

Thank you for reading this story. Leave your review. Your feedback helps me immensely!

OTHER SIMILAR BOOKS

BUNDLE - HUCOW PRISON

All the books of the Hucow Prison series with a huge discount:

1. Hucow Prison

SERIES - Auction Club

1. I'm his Property
2. He Owns Me
3. Billionaire's Fertile Risk
4. Grad Student Fertile Accident
5. Fertile Bimbo Trained
6. Owned for Being Bratty

SERIES - Fertile Only

1. Bumping the Teacher
2. Bumping the Midwife
3. Bumping the Farmhand
4. Bumping the Sinner

ABOUT THE AUTHOR

Leandra Camilli's obsession? Writing dirty, steamy stories that make her readers drool. She loves her Alpha males, hucows, sissies, and futas. If you're looking for those kinds of books, look no further.

With a cup of coffee on her table and warm socks on, she writes almost every day. Leandra Camilli has featured in several top 100 categories in the store, and she publishes weekly.